I0819505

CALLING ME HOME

CALLING ME HOME

LAURIN BECKER MACIOS

HOLIDAY HOUSE NEW YORK

This is a work of fiction. Names, characters, places, and incidents are either products of the author's imagination or, if real, are used fictitiously.

Printed and bound in March 2026 at Sheridan, Chelsea, MI, USA.
www.holidayhouse.com
First Edition
10 9 8 7 6 5 4 3 2 1
ISBN: 978-0-8234-6049-6 (hardcover)

Library of Congress Cataloging-in-Publication Data is available.

EU Authorized Representative: HackettFlynn Ltd., 36 Cloch Choirneal, Balrothery, Co. Dublin, K32 C942, Ireland. EU@walkerpublishinggroup.com

Dedicated to

TDM & RJM

with love

Be like the bird, who
Halting in his flight
On limb too slight
Feels it give way beneath him,
Yet sings,
Knowing he hath wings.

—Victor Hugo

COLORADO

AUGUST 2007

I BLINKED

and my breath
wasn't mine alone,

a plus sign appearing
on the plastic stick

in my hands.
The bedrock

of all I knew—
the very fact

of my body—
one person

in a bathroom
in a house

in a Southern Colorado town—
was suddenly untrue.

Suddenly
there were two.

JENNY?

My name
from my best friend's mouth
from the other side
of the bathroom door.

It's Rissa.

I am not big on labels,
but those two—Jenny, Rissa—
hearing them then felt, through the blur,
like some small salvation.

So why
couldn't I say
anything back?

MY MOUTH

was a collapsed
mine. I huddled

stunned under the surface
with the singular self I knew,

numb in my abruptly
foreign body—

the slumped back
of it, the folded knees

of it, the head
between its two

sweating palms.
The second

body nestled
inside of it.

I HAD ONLY BARELY

settled into this body—
its still-novel

small canyon
of B-cup cleavage,

soft hills of hip
and thigh.

I HAD ONLY BARELY

settled into this mind—
this person I'd spent

18 years becoming,
my setting

ever changing,
my friendships,

too. Discovered
facets of myself that,

brushed off and burnished
with the help

of good friends,
recalled to me

each place I'd lived
like souvenirs.

Riss had been my friend
four years—the longest

I'd lived anywhere,
known anyone.

JENNY?

Rissa called again softly,
turning the unlocked knob.

My body still, I stirred
inside it, trying

to return. Instead
I hovered above myself

like an addled shadow,
like a bird I wished

I could become.

EUROPE

JUNE 2007

UNFORGETTABLE

eyes—blue as the view
    from an airplane window

welcomed me to Rome.
    Skin as bright as the first bite

of an apple, this guy so
    unmistakably Irish.

Ciao, he greeted me
    at the hostel desk,

and something about the way
    he dipped his shoulders

in a dance as he spoke
    made my heart take flight,

his smile so big
    and pure and toothy

like sunshine calling me home.

I WON'T PRETEND

he didn't have a mullet.
He did. And a scraggly

beard, too, all of it wavy
and brown as a crisp fall leaf.

But it suited him, the sideburns,
too, framing features

so warm and comforting
he might as well have been

a campfire.

(NO CHEESY

kumbayas, no s'mores,
    just that soft

crackling sound
    you feel

in your bones
    and a heat

that wakes your body
    even as you lift

toward dreams.)

IS HE ON A GAP YEAR?

I wondered.
    He looked

roughly
    my age—

17.

IN THE NEAR-

midnight darkness,
    he checked me

into my room—
    a co-ed eight-bed

on the top floor,
    one bunk left empty

for me.

HE HELD OPEN

the heavy metal door
    as I skirted past

with my backpack,
    and asked,

You traveling alone?
    A wave of worry

rushed toward me—
    should I lie? Is he a creep?

But something in his eyes
    put me at ease,

so I let that something
    carry me. *I am.*

Damn, he said,
    looking intrigued,

then turned to leave.

FOR JUST LONG ENOUGH TO GET

where I was supposed to be,
    the narrow strip of light he'd made

held for me.

WHERE I WAS SUPPOSED TO BE

was never left to chance.
Growing up
with constant change,
I'd become my own
reliable constant.

Chart your course, hold steady
was a quote that made me *me.*
Once plan A was set,
there existed no plan B.

I'D MADE IT THROUGH HIGH SCHOOL

in one relative piece,
and with what I'd saved
from summer jobs
(Hallmark, Subway, AMC),

gifted myself this trip—a capstone—
first intended as a visit
to a few of my old homes:

the suburban London red row house
on a small street lined with bakeries, age six;

the tree-lined German lane where, age eight,
I'd plucked chestnuts, packing my square pink backpack full;

the hill in the Alps that I at twelve would fly down,
two bright summers on my bike, invincible;

then blossomed to sights
I'd researched, scheduled, set.

(IT'S INSANE

your parents
are letting you go,

my friend Foley had said,
envy in his overprotected eyes.

Not if you know them, though,
Riss had replied. Still—

It's our last summer together!
they chimed.

I need a palate cleanser,
I'd joked, unable

to explain the vague,
pressing need

I felt inside—
to bowtie this chapter—

kid-Jenny's rootless life.
Maybe I wanted

to say goodbye.
Maybe claim it as mine.)

THE PAST MONTH, THE SKY

had been mine and I'd belonged to it, too,
since peering up from the smooth steps
of Westminster Abbey. East and west,
north and south, same. I'd stood silent

at the feet of the graffitied coronation chair,
at a monument to Chaucer
erected above his bones.
I was time's and time slid

through and past and away, laughing as I'd tried
to grasp it, admire it, trembling inside it, too—
it was unlike any budding romance
with some gorgeous-souled girl or guy,

but a love so crucial I knew it as sinew,
something holding me together.
Different awe, different day—
Hadrian's Wall a wave,

all five oceans surged inside me—
and how wise and old and young and shocking
the earth they nestled was.
Different awe, different day—at Stonehenge

my body, too, was a shadow cast long
by the sun. Sharply there I felt

the mystery of what we're for.
Even the clouds seemed ancient, the grass, too—

tea and forest and lizard green,
new blades still cloistering old worlds
once teeming with people themselves dreaming, maybe,
of what was, while building their futures

stone by stone, encounter by encounter, by word
and chance and will and wish, too.

MANDATORY MESSAGE

to Mom and Dad sent
from the hostel lobby computer
(arrived safe, love you!), I slept
sounder that night than any other

on my solo trek thus far,
though the particulars
were mostly the same
as in England, Germany,

Switzerland, Belgium—
my frizzy brown hair held
in a loose bun, one arm slung
through a backpack strap,

(the bulk of it a makeshift pillow,
my belongings safe beneath my head)—
jeans still on, sweatshirt too,
asleep on my side to face

the snoring, co-ed room.

A ROMAN MONTAGE

should have played in my dreams—
my "must see" list was long:

the Colosseum, the Forum, Palatine Hill,
the Vatican, Catacombs, Pantheon.
The piazzas, the pizzas, the pasta, gelato,
the fountains, the churches, the Spanish Steps.

I had saved the best for last,
I thought—Rome and Greece—
but what I couldn't have counted on
was how over it all I'd be.

If not tired by the toll of travel—
shaky sleep, frigid showers,
sore feet—I was simply
exhausted by awe.

BUT THAT NIGHT, NEWNESS

flooded my dreams, after weeks
    of adoring all that is old—each

blackened limestone a lesson
    in my own smallness, my cog-

in-the-wheel-ness, my existence
    as a leaf on a tree.

The newness was that guy
    at check-in—the surprise

and vibe of him. How I felt:
    unbound

by autumn breeze.

FOR DAYS, ON MY WAY

to see the crumbling ancient city
    that blooms from within

a shiny modern one
    full of mopeds and gelato stands,

I tried to flirt with him—
    my first post–high school crush—

passing by check-in to ask a question
    I probably knew the answer to.

But he was nowhere to be found.

SO I DID

as I'd planned—
as the tourists do.
I immersed myself
in Rome's dual cities—
Then and Now.

Each morning,
post quick, cold,
coin-operated shower,
my wavy hair wet
on my shoulders,

I picked the day's sights
over a dry cappuccino,
noticing the froth
crackle soft on my tongue,
and split a pastry
with the pigeons.

I might have been growing travel-worn,
appreciating less about each city
as they stacked up, sight

after centuries-old sight,
homesickness slivering in,

but this morning ritual,
only its location changing,
was far from feeling old.

I, THE PERFECTIONIST,

should have loved
the Pantheon,
a building considered
by all accounts
perfect:

a perfect circle,
perfectly lit
by the perfect skylight cut
in its perfectly
constructed dome.

I stood before it my first
Roman morning, small
and ready to be amazed,
holding my pilgrim's breath
as I entered—

but I found myself
unmoved. Searching
for disorder. Some hint
of all it's been through.
The years, the shifts—

some slight crumbling.
Some stone somewhere
wearing thin. An unevenly
faded fresco. Anything . . .

I stayed a while, wanting,
then walked back into the sun.

YOU'RE JADED!

Becca said to me
back at the hostel,
her square jaw dropped
at my Pantheon talk.

Becca worked the hostel afternoons,
her shift ending about the time
I'd limp back in for the night.

We'd taken to toasting
to our days—mine full of sights,
hers full of front-desk duties,
checking us travelers in and out.

False! I laughed, slumped
on the hostel lobby's
kelly-green couch,
my sore feet crossed
on the graffitied
wooden coffee table.

T+L 4EVER!
JACKIE WAS HERE, 1999
HEIDI & EUGEN '05

The place just felt stale
as forgotten burger buns.
Too geometric, too symmetric,
too planned and perfect.

Becca rolled her brown eyes.
You've been traveling too long!

THE NEXT MORNING

Becca and I met for makeshift mimosas
in the lobby. *Cin cin*, she said, lifting

white wine topped with apple juice
in a paper water-cooler cup.

To Operation Un-Jade Jenny
and the sights we're headed to see!

To new friends! I added, glad
to have her with me.

FIRST UP, PALATINE HILL,

where domestic scenes
filled the frescoes—
a mother, bold
in blue, held
her sons; another
made a meal.

I can't wait to be a mum,
Becca said offhand,
her Aussie accent
thick as Vegemite.

Quietly I wondered
at the peace
painting the frescoes' faces,
the easy grace
of their maternal gestures,
doubtful
I'd ever feel
at home in their shoes.

Give me a decade, I said,
and I'll get back to you.

KIDS

had never featured
in my plans.
Come September I'd be studying
at NYU—the city
my gritty glamorous
backdrop—
learning a trade
chosen to keep me there:
marketing.

Perfecting the lure
of person to product, buyer
to brand, I imagined (my ten-year plan)
a leather portfolio in my hands,
full of successes that fueled me
as I dashed from cabs, shot
through skyscrapers, wandered
museums on weekends,
responsible for nobody
but me—like every
powerful woman
in every movie.

AND TRUTH BE TOLD

I wasn't sure I wanted
to skip kids like stones
into the world's polluted waves
only to hope they'd make it
to some smooth shore.

WITHOUT KIDS

what would you do?
Becca's shoulder bumped mine
as we walked through tall bright stems
of wind-waving wild grass,
through ruins.

Work, travel, I shrugged, *be me. Be free!* I crowed,
turning like a top, my open arms raking
the Palatine air, the city around us.

Becca hid her face with her hand
in half-mock embarrassment (*I'm not with her,*
she stage-whispered to a family ambling by)
then chortled—*But you're already tired of this!*

Girl, I said, *I just need a hot shower*
and an hour of bad TV.

AT THE TREVI FOUNTAIN

we cast coins that carried
our whispered wishes
into the turquoise water.

The wishes I'd tossed
across Europe splashed to mind—
in London, ten pence
for safe travels; in Munich,
a euro for the move to NYC;
a franc for my family's
happiness in Bern.

What did you wish for?
I asked Becca, lining
Oceanus in my lens.

Jenny! She turned to me,
shocked. *To share a wish*
is to waste it.

So I didn't tell her my wish—
anyway, it was so vague—

for something to be made
of the spark I'd felt
with that guy.

NEXT UP, A MUSEUM

we picked for the fun
of saying its name:
Palazzo Massimo
alle Terme.

Not gonna lie,
a museum full of statues
sounded boring
so we planned to run
quick through—

but actually
there was something
in their blank beige eyes
that felt alive.

Each spoke to me, wordless,
from its struck pose,
telling me something
about myself I hadn't known.

YOU'RE STIRRED UP

over statues? You Americans
are so confusing, Becca said
with a softhearted smirk.
It's just a woman sprawled
on a couch. She chuckled,
eyeing the figure before us,

and she was right—it was
just a woman sprawled
on a couch. I said so
and smiled, but my noodle heart
pulsed harder, feeling things
I couldn't name.

I WANTED THE TOUCH

of every sleek surface—
supple drape of marble togas,
lithe limbs the women lifted,
stuck for centuries in repose
or movement, frozen in time
but gliding along with it,
of the past, but present, too.

Time felt lighter—the way it laced
their carved fingers without consequence,
bounced off a broken toe, a riven arm,
and I was rooted, and I was rising,
a green bud bright beyond the doors.

(I WASN'T THINKING

about high school,   how its heartbreaks
hardly held up against   this tangible
example of Time—   bullied for my
unruly hair, stink-eyed   by cliques—and sometimes
cared—but the stuff   that really crushed me:
the senior welcome party,   its blur of beer
and tears, my skin still fire   at the memory; or
Mom and Dad hounding me   after reading my diary,
learning I loved a girl,   learning that holding
her soft hand under the table   of science lab was no experiment
but something that made   my sophomore heart erupt.
I still hear *bisexual*   like I heard it from their mouths—
though they put the emphasis   on *sexual*, I heard that love
could be bifurcated,   worried I was split in two—
one Jenny my parents liked,   and one they didn't.)

LATER THAT NIGHT

I spun the best
spaghetti of my life
on my fork
in the run-down restaurant next
to the hostel, refilled
my house red,
and finally said
what had been
on my mind awhile.

So, when I checked in
it was with this guy . . .
mullet, beard, brown hair, blue eyes . . .
but I haven't seen him since . . .

THAT'D BE COLIN

Becca replied
without batting an eye,
almost like she knew my wish.

Unearthing a crinkled
schedule from her purse,
she paired her grin with a wink.

He's on holiday till Tuesday,
then back at it
with his graveyard shift.

BUT BY TUESDAY,

two days away, I'd be gone,
on to my next adventure—
the holy grail of which I'd long dreamed,
for years internally bowing
to its figurative feet—Greece.

Oh well, I shrugged, wilted,
willing a smile. *I guess it wasn't*
meant to be. I knew I knew nothing

about him and figured
I'd get over the feeling fast—
that unexplainable sense
that he wasn't yet in the past.

ON MY STORMY MORNING FLIGHT TO ATHENS

the flight attendant held a newspaper
toward my shaking hand, which I'd managed
to unclasp from the arm of the seat—no small feat.

Likely she thought reading could help me
forget we were bolting through the sky
in a metal bottle. I flipped the news to find

the front-page headline: PLANE CRASH;
NONE SURVIVED. I mouthed a prayer
the rest of the ride, my eyes on the image of Greece

in the seatback before me—a caryatid,
calm as could be, her stone toga windless,
holding a temple on top of her head.

WHEN I WAS LITTLE, I LOVED

flying. Turbulence
    was a particular treat—

I loved the idea
    of the wind beneath my feet,

the *bounce, bump, clunk*
    of the clouds,

the scream of the engine—loud—
    as we soared high with goodbyes,

the murmur and moan as we dipped
    low to land—hello.

I'm not sure just when or why
    that changed—somewhere

I realized the room
    for human error.

Almost overnight,
    planes, trains, boats,

if I needed to take them,
    could keep me up at night.

But still, I'd take them,
telling myself that fear

is the bud of bravery,
that only from it

can a full flower bloom.

SINCE TOUCHING DOWN A MONTH AGO

at Heathrow, I hadn't flown.
Solely to make the leap
from Rome to Greece,

I'd planned to fly, to make the most
of time's quick tick
in the classic pillars of antiquity.

An adventure, yes, but I was cautious
as could be, fingers always crossed
that I make it to my dreams—

NYU, NYU, NYU.

OPA!

was the soundtrack
to my Athenian hostel,
a jam-packed tavern in the lobby.

Ouzo practically oozing
from my pores, I cheersed—
ya mas!—and cheersed—
ya mas!—my fellow travelers.

The times I drank before this trip
could be counted on one hand—
two homecomings, one prom,
and the party I tried to forget.

The past five weeks, when alone
in a crowd, I'd allowed myself
one drink. But there I was,
my last week, finally in Greece.
I breathed a sigh of relief and let
my tired guard down. Anyway,
this hostel's rooms were not co-ed.
My brand-new friends and I danced
like dorks, our arms linked. Laughter
cramped my cheeks. *Opa!*

We were zealots—drunk
on beer, booze, freedom—
and in love with the moment.

Adventure addicts and culture buffs—*ya mas!*
Language freaks and dharma bums—*ya mas!*
Spring breakers and bucket-listers—*ya mas!*

My guard was tired.
My guard was down.

Opa.

THAT NIGHT THE GUY

working the front desk followed me upstairs

hands reaching   eyes rasping

up the unending white stairwell winding

leaving me winded as I reached the heavy hall door

to the girls' floor   barricading myself behind it

three girls nearby not thinking twice

rolling from bed to help me hold the door

our four bodies straining

till thankfully some other guy walked by

and he drifted   nonchalantly   away

THAT WAS A CLOSE ONE!

one of my new friends laughed.

Meanwhile, even my hair
was shaking.

MORNING CAME BRIGHT

and soon. My brain buzzed as I trudged
out of the hostel and around the corner
to peer up at the temple of temples,
the ruins I'd dreamed of seeing for years—
the Parthenon standing proud atop the Acropolis.

There was already a crowd, but I didn't mind
moving slow. I had nowhere else to go, just a goal
of communing with the caryatids, of letting
my eyes wander among the milk-white stones
that dotted the wild grass—lime-green, overgrown,
sun-yellow blooms holding their own against
the Mediterranean breeze.

I sat on a stone bench, drinking in
the temple's crumbling columns stacked piece
by ever-aging piece. Athens itself bewitched me,
the foaming sea of its white low-rises
lapping at the lip of storied green hills—and the sky,
blue-gray and speckled with clouds that shifted
stoically from one shape to the next.

MY MIND WAS THERE, AMONG THE CLOUDS,

when a voice broke in and brought me
back to Greece, to the ancient hilltop
beneath my feet. *Hi pretty girl,* the voice said.
Pretty girl? . . . Pretty girl. I scanned the ground
for the stray dog or brown bird the voice was beckoning,
then realized the call was meant for me.

Instant inventory of my energy stores read: nil.
Zero to chitchat, zilch to connect,
zip to deflect. So I gave him—
this handsome, crisp, twice-my-age guy—
the universal shrug-and-smile with
apologetic eyes that said, *Sorry,*
I don't speak your language.

I thought he'd fold his map back up
and leave—naïve. His mouth a sky
unleashing lightning, I rushed to what I hoped
was safety—the museum doors. My smile
a shield I clung to, he kept step
berating me, his jilted breath on my neck,
and I saw from the corner of my eye
his grin growing knowing I understood
the violence of every word he slung at me.

INSIDE

I sat on a museum bench
feeling empty
as a hotel drawer.

Silence poured from the shut mouths
of ancient statues
who had seen girls
in much worse shape
than me.

I know, I thought.

But still, what did I have but my one
pulsing body, my one
worn mind, to live in?

Slowly a thread
in the drawer's corner
came into focus—

the feeling
that I was lucky
to be feeling anything.

Grab that thread,
the statues seemed
to want to say.
But how?

AND THEN–THE QUESTION

of when to leave the building.

Stay till night could cover me
in her dark dress? But I knew night,
like day, was indifferent—
she would cover him, too.

I left in the light, inserting myself
in a school group tour, grateful for once
for looking like a child.

THE THREE GIRLS–

New Yorkers, as it happened,
sent to Greece for high school graduation—
were in their bunks when I got back.

Hey bitch, the blond one said
as I collapsed on my bed. *Day go better*
than your night?

My skin snake-slicked, I prickled
at *bitch.* I took a moment to breathe,
to tell myself that this time it was friendly.

Surprisingly similar, I said. *But with a side*
of ancient scenery.

Well, we're headed off to island-hop
in the morning if you want to come.
Get some sun?

I COULD HAVE SWORN THAT NIGHT

I didn't sleep, yet I dreamed a map—
one marked with all my plans—
was crumbling in my grip.

When the sun rose, I did the same,
fidgeting my fingers against
my bottom lip as I waited my turn
for the hostel's lone computer.

Don't freak, but . . . I think in Greece
I'll just lay on the beach. One ruin's
the same as the next, I wrote
in a note to Mom and Dad. *Off to Mykonos,*
Naxos, Santorini—still home next week as planned.

THE ISLANDS

were windy, welcoming,
each rising from the teal water
like a parent with open arms.
Stepping onto their shores
felt like being loved—the tide,
the sand, the breeze, the easy
stucco shops and restaurants,
locals' soft smiles, whether wide
or just at the edges.

We docked last at Santorini,
drove streets curly as grape vines
to the tip-top town of Oia—a place
whose quiet grace pinched my throat.
Santorini was not just somewhere.
It was someone I wanted to become.

IN SANTORINI WE STUMBLED

upon a bookshop that seemed
like a special secret, a cave carved
into the island's stark white walls.

A soft Southern drawl drifted
from behind the desk, a guy
glancing up to greet us,
The Dubliners open
and dog-eared in his lap.

I browsed, breathing in the scent
of old books laced with beach breeze,
my fingers grazing the shelved spines.

I lingered when the girls left for lunch,
and learned: *Dylan, 23, Tennessee,*
opened the shop with his friend two years back.

Wowed, envious, I wondered out loud—
So, you live on the island?

In silence he stood and walked
to the shop's curved corner
where his fingers found a knot of twine
between two shelves. Fiddling it loose,
the shelves parted to reveal a bed.
He pointed past where I stood astonished—
Back there is the kitchen.

OY!

rang a velvet voice, bright as the woman trailing it
through an arched doorway, her pear-sized biceps,

one enthralling violet vein awake with the strain
of a slipping stack of books. I cocked my head to look—

The Country Girls, Infinite Jest, The Wayward Bus, Leaves of Grass,
Lunch Poems, Dream Work, The Unabridged Journals of Sylvia Plath.

She held the books toward me and I took them, as I took in
her bare fingers dusting off her white ribbed tank, tight

on her small tan frame, her baggy cut-off denim frayed
along her freckled thighs. *This is my co-owner,* Dylan said.

Maggy, she whispered, winking a long-lashed eye, its
shimmering iris a spill of cinnamon-speckled coffee.

And actually, he's my *co-owner.* The left side of her long lips—
tinged red as a scratched bite—lifted as she offered her hand.

I shifted the stack of books to my hip,
felt something in me shimmy as I shook it.

SHELVE THOSE

and stay for a bite to eat?

Task complete, Maggy waved me—*follow Dyl*—
toward spiral steps that vanished
through the graffitied ceiling, led

to a sunlit rooftop terrace
with a view of the island's half moon,
the volcano it spoons in sparkling cerulean water.

She joined us with a wafting cyan platter of pita,
a teal bowl of homemade tirokafteri.
I worked to be sly as I watched her

watch the water be still beneath us,
as I watched her watch the sky stay blue.
I head home tomorrow for a family reunion, she said—

and hate to leave Dyl all week, but no one we know is free . . .
I wonder, she said. *Would you be amenable?* she asked . . .
Right place, right time, Dylan laughed.

I SURPRISED MYSELF

by saying goodbye to the girls,
by staying at the shop, but it was
too amazing an offer to let drop.

I lived among books
all week, my bed a loft
accessible by a handmade ladder
(four stones strapped to a plank
of wide wood) in the back room—
the room reserved for art, plays, poetry,
and Brizo, the beloved bookshop mutt.

I helped at the desk in exchange
for room and board, but I also had time
to be lazy. I tried to read the greats,
plucking them one by one off the shelf,
starting, stopping, switching.
My brain and body were blank
as a brand-new journal. I was resting,
but I wore worry like lotion, around Dylan
especially, sharing this space just us two.
(He seemed harmless, kindhearted,
but my senses were stuck on high alert.)

Then one afternoon as I waited
outside the corner gyro shop
for sinfully good falafel loaded
with thick fries and tangy tzatziki,

I noticed a book abandoned on a stretch
of that famous Oia white wall.
I checked it out—worn, waterlogged,
Ann Brashares and her magical jeans.

That's literary contraband, Dylan squeamed when I got back,
his face a prune. *Have me arrested,* I said,
tossing it on my bed for later.

FAST FRIENDS

Dylan and I were not; we butted heads a lot.
I laughed at the literal shrine he'd built
his adopted namesake, Bob, despite (father's
daughter that I am) knowing the songs
like the back of my hand, and despite Dylan
disclosing he'd changed his name at 18
to be more like the man himself, then learned
the tambourine.

And he couldn't stand that I knew
which Gossip Girl was who, had inhaled the series
countless times. *You know you love me,* I called after him
the night he huffed in disgust toward his bed of books,
enraged I could say I'd take *Dumb and Dumber*
over *Requiem for a Dream* any day. (*You seem so mature
till you're exactly your age*, he gibed,
to which I pantomimed, with relish, *barf.)*

So it was unexpected, to say the least,
that thanks to him I found, then released,
a locked latch inside me.

IT WAS THE ANNUAL DAY

all of Oia, brushes and buckets in hand,
rewhitened the ribbon walls streaming
from sky to sand. Sun-cheeked, paint-smudged,
Dylan and I ate our block's communal
cookout together—lamb, feta, olives on a spit—
and I shared my plate with a stray. Dylan
didn't approve; a spat ensued. I remember only the end.

You're proud, he said.

You're pretentious, I replied.

Our faces were two stones in the same wall, till,
struck, his crumbled soft as lime. *I am?* he said.
I don't want to be.

My tongue froze above my defenses, adrenaline
prickling my skin. Giving an accusation
consideration? Not simply as a reflex raising
figurative fists? The concept, to me, was foreign.
I was floored. I slept on it, half-dreams circling
the fuzzy understanding—that this is what he meant.

At sunrise I shuffled, sleep-heavy, into the kitchen,
saying before I could stop myself, *I might be proud.*
I'm not proud of it.

The hangnail moon still strung in the pale sky,
Dylan's lips took the uncertain curve of its slim
saltwater reflection. He handed me a fat slice
of spanakopita, said, *Maybe we'll both be cooler people today.*

ON MY DAY OFF

I rode the bookshop bike down winding roads to the beach.
Greece was on my mind, heavy with the weight it held
my whole life, ever since my third-grade class studied it.
That was my first year living in Germany, and the kids there
hated me. *Ausländer raus,* they chanted at recess—*foreigner,*
get out—they followed me home.

What could I do? I traveled past them into the ancient myths
I held in my hands. I hung out with Hera, Athena, Apollo; I hid
behind Agamemnon's mask; I turned myself to stone, struck still
as a caryatid, untouchable and strong.

Finally, all those years later, I was there. I wanted to care,
but I found myself snapped as a shell, like the ones pressing
their shapes into my skin. The Greek black sand hugged
my wet body like a glove. I sent a silent, half-assed hello
to Helios, Greek god of the sun, as he soaked me,
cold tea numbing my tongue.

BEACH-WARM AND WAKING

from the daze of sand-strewn dreams
I saw that guy—Colin?—clear as day
walking the water's edge. Only of course
it was someone else instead. I wondered—
had Colin given me a second thought?

I rolled over, plucking Feist from my ears,
and grabbed the contraband Ann
from my bag. *Worth a try . . .*

The book was my balm. I devoured it,
finally forgetting myself in its story,
my worries a cloud changing shape
from Mount Olympus into something
I could carry.

WHAT'S YOUR PLAN FROM HERE?

Dylan asked one night, a silent film in black and white
projected on the shop's back wall. *Duh*—I raised
my brows—*NYU*—like he already knew,
shocked to learn he didn't. I'd lived there near a week
and not talked—not even *thought*—about it,
for the first time in years. *Whoa,* I said,
our twin grins arching. He nudged my knee, said,
Living in the moment. Feels good, right?
I grabbed the popcorn, rolled my smiling eyes.

IT WAS THE END OF MY STAY,

my flight home to the States just
one day away, when I looked up
from my book's final page. I sat back
inside myself, sipping my gritty Greek coffee,
feeling at peace. Sure, I hadn't really
"seen" Greece, but someday I'd come back
and do it right. Life was long. The next day,
as scheduled, I'd leave—first stop,

Athens airport; next stop, home base,
as I'd begun to think of Mom and Dad's,
for the rest of my glorious summer,
planned jobless to spend with
Mom, Dad, soon-scattering friends
(Riss to Boulder for nursing,
Foley to Boston for business)—
before moving to NYU.

SUDDENLY, SHUFFLING BODIES

snapped me back to the outdoor café,
a hurried crowd pressed against
the low white terrace wall.

I followed a man's pointed finger to find
a cruise ship cradled in the island's arms,
careening, leaning, losing herself in the water.

Baby boats slid from her belly toward shore.
Everyone watched, shocked. Time pretended
to stop. Eventually *All passengers safe!* a waiter called

from indoors, his ear to a radio. The air
seemed to shake, a wave of breath unbound.

THE SUN SPILLED THAT EVENING

like wine across the bookshop terrace
where Dylan and I sat drinking cheap red
from stemless flutes, disagreeing
on everything, laughing here and there,
watching the sun, the ship, disappear.

That night each wooden tock
of the bookshop's clock was present
in my shadowed dreams, ticking me closer
to my own ferry, my flight.

At twilight, off to catch my boat,
Dylan woke to remind me *Two ships*
won't sink this week. My laugh a puff
of morning air, we goodbye high-fived.

IT WASN'T UNTIL I ARRIVED

with a tired sigh at my airport gate

having slept most of the way

that I learned from a paper strewn

on the seat beside me:

Father And Daughter Dead In Santorini Shipwreck

I FELT NUMB

and dumb
thinking of their pain,
their loss,
the void
an unseen arm
of the sea floor created,
the ship brushing against it
by mistake.

Good afternoon, passengers. We are now boarding
American Airlines Flight 285.

I'd sat watching
a scene almost serene,
thinking all were safe.
Everyone—
locals, tourists, me,
we went back to talking,
laughing, watching
casually. But two lives
were ending.

All zones are now welcome to board.

By the grace
of god or some stroke
of luck or sheer

random happenstance,
I was fine
and they
were not.
That was our lot.

This is the final boarding call for American Airlines Flight 285.

Life was only long if you were lucky.

My body rose and led me, like a friend
taking my hand. But it didn't head for the gate.

It threw my ticket in the trash
and walked the other way.

I FOUND MYSELF

in a blink, slack-jawed, sitting
in the overgrown grass
of the Greek Agora.

My pack warm against my back,
I watched the apricot sun slide
slow across the sky—but of course
it was me moving, Earth's smooth spin
dependable enough to go forgotten.

I FOUND MYSELF

a ripple in a seaway, pulled
by thoughts of Dad and Mom, how
our lives seemed like the ocean—together

in the deep, ebbing slowly
to shore, where drops inescapably sink
into hot sand, or catch

in halved shells, or gather
in shallow pools
where small fish circle

in the sunlight.
How I missed them.
How I was glad to know

they were there.

DUSK YAWNED

pink as a newborn,
and it dawned on me—I had no plan.
No hostel bed awaited. No ticket
bore my name. In fact, not a soul
could say where I was. Well—the couple
sitting nearby, but they didn't know I was "I."
I was no one here to anyone but me—
a feeling, I thought, I could get used to.

A line I'd read somewhere
blew in on the breeze—
I will never know a single thing anyone feels,
just how they say it.
I tilled the soil around that, then
grabbed a literal fistful, feeling
ageless crumbs of earth
warm themselves in my palm.

Later I found an internet café
to log on and let Mom and Dad know
the plan had changed—
though what it was, I couldn't say.

But a notification distracted me . . .

HEY

read the whole note
    sent through MySpace.

One small word greeting me
    next to a photo of him—

Colin. A bird in my chest swooped
    low to the ocean's edge,

soared toward watercolor clouds
    while I bathed in the sight

of the letters of his name
    and replied with the same small

hey.

I CLICKED THROUGH

photo after photo
    of his smile shining

like a half moon knocked
    sideways by its own brightness,

eyes warm as stars above it.
    I gleaned what I could:

When not in Rome
    he lived in a turquoise house

in Doolin, County Clare,
    with *Mam* and *Da*

and a sister, maybe two?
    He surfed—one shot

of his body balanced,
    pearlescent, on top

of a wave, gliding sure
    as a gull through air.

I mirrored smile
    after captured smile,

lingered on one photo
    of a straight face—

head tilted toward his short
        mam's shoulder, one thin arm

squeezing her close,
        a farm, maybe? a field? the ocean

wide behind them.

MEANWHILE

night was falling fast. I opened a humbling map
on my greasy blue-and-white-checkered place mat
while downing dolmas in a little diner.

There was still so much to see.

I made half plans—this country, that town.
I'd find room and board when I arrived
or feast on transit—the in-between, unable
to label my local, sleeping on overnight trains,
sojourning with starlight.

I rode this second wind straight
to the train station ticket window asking
Where's the train taking me tonight?

HUNGARY WAS THE ANSWER

but the night had other ideas for me,
the Budapest-bound train screeching
to a halt in a field around midnight.
I jolted awake to the sharp shapes
of three uniformed men, their seashell skin
blossoming shrimp-pink, jagged words
I couldn't grasp blaring from their mouths.

Luck was with me in the form of a lady
who not so much translated
as pleaded on my behalf.

They want me to get off the train? I asked,
their gestures unmistakable, steel guns glinting
at their hips.

I stretched my trembling ticket toward them.
An officer took it, tore it twice.
The pieces twirled to his boots.

They're try to bribe you, the woman said.
They want thousands and say they will leave you here,
but don't pay. Seronjo—they're assholes,
bunch of assholes!

I tried to look out the window
to see where I was about to end up
but it was a blank black wall of night.

She convinced them I'd get cash
at the next stop, and in the relative silence
as the train cut the sky, I thought about why
they'd picked me. I'd thought I seemed
to be traveling with nothing—
my high school Jansport jammed
with a jacket, spare pair of jeans, extra shirt,
face wash, underwear, iPod, book.
The sore thumb of my presence itself
hadn't yet occurred to me. Briefly,
I wondered what and who
those three men went home to,
then sank back to sleep.

My dear, the woman shook my shoulder
as we slowed, hours later, into a station.
When doors open, run. Do not come back
to these assholes. Take the next train!

Hvala, I thanked her, our lips upturned
as we clasped quick hands in a covert goodbye.

TWELVE HOURS TO WAIT, I FELL IN LOVE

with Beograd. One and the same, in America
we call it Belgrade. Both feel like nicknames
for a place I think of first as a feeling, second
as a series of images, third by its name.

It was so early nothing was open.
Sitting on the gum-pocked sidewalk,
I scanned the city's small section in my guidebook.
One hostel listed, but wherever it was, I was not—
I circled nearby blocks for naught, thinking
I'd stay the night, then gave up.

I walked down cobblestone streets, popped
into steaming bakeries, rested on stone benches
in magenta sun. I saw no souvenir shops,
no internet cafés, met no one along my path
all day who spoke English.

A fresh-made member of the Beograd Library
to use the internet, I read a reply from Mom
and Dad—*Have you lost your mind?!*
What have you done with our daughter?!,
then, with held breath opened a message from Colin

that crept and curled into my heart
like a cat in a cupboard.

Walking back outside, the city's soul pulsed
blue as a crayon-drawn sky against crowds
of fuchsia tulips. I was floating in that city
that felt like a friend, a friend who so understood me
we needn't speak.

HE HAD THOUGHT OF ME, TOO,

he said, home in Ireland
with his childhood view,

green hills pocked bright
with yellow gorse,

the ocean glimmering
and frothy in the wind.

He had pictured me there—
thought he'd seen me

reading on a ledge
near the edge of town,

alone on the cliffs
where he walked

each morning, routine steps
in spring dew

before the familiar rain
of afternoon.

I don't know why, he wrote,
but you've been stuck

in my mind's eye—I figured
you'd have forgotten me,

if ever I was someone
you'd noticed enough

to forget. But when I got back
to the Lemon, Becca said

the American backpacker
who'd become her friend

had asked about me.

ON AN ISLAND BENEATH A BRIDGE

that connects Buda and Pest, halved pieces
    of the capital, east and west, I sat the next day
eating a Hungarian lunch, cool cottage cheese

spiced and speckled with radish. I thought about bridges—
    first literal, then not. How at one time
they weren't built, didn't yet do the work

of quick connection, two places so near each other
    so split. I walked from site to sacred site,
the sun softening into the other side of the earth,

then cloaked myself in the rich maroon velvet
    of a tea house, a hot ceramic pot steeping,
then steaming—smelling like sweet, damp spring—

into my clear glass mug. The next day I'd check
    my inbox in whatever city welcomed me
off the evening train. For a while longer that night,

the air incensed with Hungarian folk songs,
    I mused, grateful for other people,
their brains and abilities, for time that links

their visions together, so that complex notions
    become simple pleasures to me—
a bridge. An email. A cup of tea.

IN SLOVENIA

I knocked on the door of distant family
I'd met once before, when I was ten.
That was when we lived in Poland
and traveled on weekends.

We'd driven there then—a treasure hunt—
armed with gestures, a dictionary,
a few marriage records, asking for the family
with my mom's maiden name,

until through word-of-mouth
we found them
in a tiny ten-house town
in the woods

beautiful in its silence
near a river so see-through
you could count the gray stones at its base,
the soft fish swimming above them.

WE CANOED AGAIN

all those years later,
on the River Kolpa,
my cousin-of-sorts and I.

Dropping our oars, we let
the current guide us past
our family's empty red mill,
my cousin's umber eyes
round as stones.

I noticed my body ache
with what had been set aside—
the weight of the oar, of the water.

IT FELT LIKE MORE

than mere weeks before
that I'd arrived in Germany
unaware of what I'd find,
of what I was looking for.

Ach yes, just what the world needs—
another American backpacker
searching for herself, a cute
German waiter had said.

What a dick, I'd thought,
as I smiled and ordered a Coke.
But it'd got me thinking, as I squeezed
the lemon wedge he'd brought me
into the neck of the thin glass bottle.

Was I searching for myself?
Was I wishing there was a place,
some elusive Home, where all
my memories awaited me?
A worn banister to slide me toward
a forgotten Christmas morning?
A dead moth dotting my windowsill
to send me back to the sweltering state fair?
(I loved the wind against my face
in that little wooden roller coaster . . .)

Or the sweet mildewy scent
of my parents' packed bookshelf
to plunk me back on our cozy couch
post-dinner? Maybe I was.

But then, I'd thought, a sweet sip sparkling
on my tongue, wasn't I remembering
those things anyway, as it was,
sitting there in a metal chair
on the sidewalk of a random bratwurst shop,
snowflakes hinting at themselves
in the gray-quartz clouds?

IN THE GULF OF PIRAN,

the sea mist slick on my skin,
    I turned 18.

I sent Colin a photo
    of myself in the salt flats,

a secret diamond of sea salt slowly
    dissolving against my tongue.

Above it I typed the feeling
    that was crystallizing in me—

that everyone and everything
    seemed like salt, formed

by dissipating days and years
    that left us ultimately to ourselves

or to who and what would have us,
    having already a million times over

moved on, creating, creating.
    It felt dark, seeing it written,

but the bright salt briny
    in my hands was beautiful,

tasted like the sun.

MESSAGES BETWEEN

Colin and me
    became lush, deep,

steady. I was as alone
    as I'd ever be—

a small brown bird
    landing, lifting, landing—

but I felt Colin threaded
    into every city

by whichever message
    met me there—each

capricious stop feeling
    just like Colin:

totally random,
    meant to be. Surprising

inevitability.

IN CROATIA

the walls of Old Dubrovnik
    lifted me toward the ancient sun, led me along
        the time-proven path of the shore.

        The water's glistening stung my eyes,
    but I tried to hold my gaze, the view
almost a view of time itself.

Wrapped in my own arms,
    I listened for the sound of the sun
        setting on the horizon,

        but it was the walls who spoke first,
    their battle scars held
at the surface.

THERE, MY HEARTBREAKS

crashed open—cold waves
at my feet—their presence,
each so different, crested
on the same sea.

Crowded, I slid a song
into my ears—Anna Nalick, "Catalyst."

I wondered if I'd ever be over them,
if wounds would fade to scars
on my symbolic self-portrait statue.

Cory, whom I didn't kiss
at the end of our freshman year date,
declaring me *too pale*
to be pretty.

Lisa, who rang our bell, tenth grade,
her mom's car idling angrily
in the road, pressing rushed kisses
to my lips, my palm. *Boarding school,*
she said, *I'll write you.* Never did.

Jeremy. The senior welcome party
blaring in his basement. Jeremy
taking my virginity
while I said *please no.*

THE WEEKEND AFTER IT HAPPENED

I told my parents I was sick,
wrapped my body's razor ache

in my fake-down duvet.
She's lifeless, Foley'd whispered

to Riss, probably more audibly
than intended, the two of them

the only ones who knew.
Maybe you need to cry,

Riss offered, the second day they sat
at my bedside, my dry eyes boring holes

through nothing. I moved
only when Riss touched a tender

black bruise peeking its fat
finger shape from my shirt sleeve,

when Foley saw it and breathed
I'll kill him. But none of us

did anything. We felt
the days spin slow—

or I did. We felt ourselves small—
or I did, loosened

in the planet's spinning
grip, its questionable

hold. Monday
at school, I saw him, his

Crest-confident smile, his
strut toward my locker, his

high-pitched high fives—startling—his
wide thighs   his

wide biceps   the weight
of his torso   I felt it   his

gait   his   grin   his   Tommy-tinged
sweat   his   unaffected air splitting

the atoms between us as he
stepped toward me standing

softly   still bruised   at my locker
as he said   *Hey Campbell—*

my last name—   in the voice he'd used
for months to say   *I love you*

and I turned away   and that was it—
he did too   as smoothly as if

he'd never walked toward me
as if there was somewhere else

he'd meant to go   still smiling
neither of us ever speaking

to each other   another word.

(I HAD GOOD EXES, TOO,

for the record, ones
it didn't hurt to remember,
recalling them easy as ocean
to sand—

Angie, who held my hand
along the Mind Eraser's plummets
and loops;

Luke, who offered his lap
so long it must've gone numb
when all the theater seats were full;

Ray, who slept with the phone
on his pillow for weeks
after I read *The Shining*
and was scared to fall asleep—

so when bad ones sprang to mind,
I summoned them instead, their care
as pure and comforting as fog.)

DUBROVNIK'S SHIMMERING STAIRS

in sun-draped drizzle led me
    to a dark, empty café where Colin—

black letters, white screen
    on a canary-yellow computer—

asked me to come back.
    Come again and see me, hey,

before you head all the way home?
    The stairs led me down

to the Onofrio fountain
    where sixteen stone faces,

for centuries, offered water
    from a nearby spring.

I leaned toward the fountain,
    thoughtless of a wish, cool water

cascading on my tongue.

QUICKLY

I was running out of travel funds,
the money I'd saved working
each summer since turning fourteen.

At a mirror moment last year,
Becca took her boss's advice—
This doesn't need to be an "adventure"
before you go back to your "real life"—
if you love this life, make it real.

I turned that idea, like smooth sea glass,
over often, trying to figure whether this life,
some version of it, could be for me—unplanned,
unconventional, open to chance, carefree—
but NYU—the future I'd envisioned
since I was old enough to dream—was waiting.
(Plus, Mom and Dad, already semi-fuming,
would surely freak.)

Meanwhile, it was all overnight trains—
the cost of a hostel cut out—
and grocery store baguettes torn
open and stuffed with cheese.

I DECIDED TO GIVE MYSELF

one more week (*and that's IT!*
Mom and Dad agreed). One more week
to visit Colin and, this time, do Rome right.
Last time I'd been a California poppy
come night, petals shut tight
awaiting sun.

By way of a speeding bus
through the bald Bosnian mountains,
I circled to Split, then boarded
a broken-down joke of a ferry
to Italy, where I'd catch a train.

The Adriatic sweeping me
off my feet and closer to Colin,
I crossed my fingers and stared out
at the sea's blurry breath—longing
suspended in the air
like a freshly-sung string of vowels.
My sea-floor fears fogged a bit
behind lesser worries—

Would it be weird to see him?
Would what we felt break
like blown glass when we met again
face-to-face, the temperature in the air
shifting out of cyberspace?

IT WAS 4 A.M.

when my train whistled into Rome,
a high and hopeful sound

that will always send me back
to schlepping my pack off the train,

my hair pure grease, my clothes, too—
to spot Colin asleep on a bench, a cheesy

clear-wrapped red rose sweetly
tucked beneath his arm.

I woke him with a shoulder poke
and when he saw me, the smile

that painted his face was an otherwise
undiscovered masterpiece—

Michelangelo, da Vinci, Pasquini . . .
When he stood, our fingers touched

and I felt—quickly, a flash—the feeling
from the Agora, the lush earth

revealing herself to me.

SITTING STILL AS STONE BUDDHAS

on the outskirts of the Forum, we shared
a sweet maritozzo, our legs dangling

from an ancient marble wall.
The sun rose like a silky spoonful

of gelato, then melted, flooding
the famous landscape in lemon light.

The spot where Caesar was cremated
burst with flowers bright as blood.

I was full of feathers. Soft plumes,
sharp quills. And I could fly—

a bird—or drop—a pillow on a bed.
Next to me, the promise of Colin.

Around me in every direction,
proof that nothing lasts.

How many hands have brushed
this old stone wall? I said, mostly

for something to say.
Yeah . . . he stared, contemplative . . .

And how many butts? The ice
broke loud beneath our laughter.

INCHES OF AIR, ELECTRIC

between us, we circled the Colosseum.
Colin stopped short

under an ancient archway,
throngs of tourists jostling by.

Staring into my eyes, he raised
his hand as for a high five. Mine

met his, our palms two sheets
of paper. I felt a love note

scrawling itself between them.
In a beat, we laced our fingers

and entered the famous maze
of stairways and corridors,

trap doors and disappearing floors—
from then on intertwined.

LATER, REFRESHED

by my first shower in eight days, we met
for his night off (requested and granted

for my visit) outside the Lemon lobby doors.
He'd tucked away two paychecks

to take me for pasta, *prego,* wine, dessert—
a dinner that out-fancied prom (though Foley,

Riss, and I had done it right)—then we'd club
with Becca and Colin's hostel crew. I worried

dinner would be awkward, but the few gaps
in conversation felt natural, time to sip and savor

each other. More than wine, I drank him in
from across the small square table—

airy gestures, singsong voice, listening eyes.
By dessert, my heart was all ambrosial ache,

creamy panna cotta on a spoon. Colin's arm
around me tight, we stepped out into

the starry night and stopped, spotlit
at the curb by a streetlight. We laughed,

not knowing or caring why, our faces close.
Our mouths became two moths

with lifted wings, each other's lips
the only lights in Rome.

THAT WEEK WE TRAIPSED,

obnoxious lovers, through the city,
link-armed and lousy with kisses.

I could have sworn the sun, the moon,
were lanterns lit for us. We followed them

down cobblestone side streets
just to see where they would lead.

WE FOUND OURSELVES

one late afternoon, underground in a chapel,
surrounded by walls of skulls, urged to see

our bodies for the bones they are—foundations
for our lives, for what will later be built by people

who will struggle to even imagine us
as having been real. *Bleak shite,* Colin whispered,

his wide grin warm against my ear, his beard's
soft scratch on my cheek. He made the sign

of the cross as we left—*bless 'em*—
touched a kiss, like a wafer, to my tongue.

IN THE SISTINE CHAPEL

spellbound
by the near-touch

of the tips
of their fingers

in that cracked
and colorless sky,

we craned
our necks,

standing chest
to chest

as though a vow
might pass

between us,
hands clasped

like lockets,
mesmerized.

HOW CAN I PUT THIS?

We found an empty room
or made one of Palatine grass.

Our bodies became caves
on the ocean's edge.

We lost ourselves, ecstatic
inside them, then

waded slow toward stars—
flecks of ancient light

in the onyx night nudging us
to the naked shore.

NEVER HAD I EVER

had a nickname
till I became

his Little J.
I felt adored,

inevitably his,
the way

a river might feel
in the rain.

THE DUNGEON

Colin's room was called—twelve twin basement beds,
bunked for Lemon employees. One lightbulb

on a string, graffiti gracing everything, the smell
of ever-suitcased, unwashed clothes mingled

with whiffs of mint soap. I crashed there though
the boss made me buy a bed down the hall.

While Colin worked, I slept. In the morning, he'd
catch up on Z's, me beside him, reading, barely needing

the book anymore—Whitman's *Leaves of Grass*
brought with me from home. I knew each word

to my favorite poems—"A Noiseless Patient Spider,"
"Song of the Open Road." But I read them anyway—

filament, filament, filament casting itself
from me toward Colin, toward Rome,

and finally, toward what I thought of as home.
Then he'd wake and off we'd go—a cappuccino, a trek,

the sites, the city our playground till it burst, blood orange,
announcing the approach of another night.

OUR BODIES A BASKET

braided on the Spanish Steps,
we wove our stories, too.

Him: raised at the lip
of the Atlantic with

his older sister Emer
and his beloved surfboard

to the strum of cláirseach,
the whistle of flute—

his da and mam's Irish music.
Set to study, undeclared, at Trinity

he'd landed in Roma months before
on a gap year, where his future

flashed on like a bulb:
open a hostel back home.

Me: my transient, only-child
childhood trailing my dad's job

(global HR consulting, taken
for the travel) while Mom

worked freelance web design
and took care of me;

my nascent wonder
of the word *home.* My plans:

marketing maven in the city
that never sleeps—

the profession picked
because it seemed so

New York—
the city, partly,

for how many people there
are from *elsewhere*.

MARKETING, YEAH?

Colin said
out of thin air one day,

tucking a wave of hair
behind my ear.

We were lounging
on the Lemon lobby couch

talking to Becca.
I can't see it. He shook his head.

I laughed. I knew
I agreed—this trip

had changed
or revealed me,

but this me
felt so new, my plans

so long. I grinned.
Guess you don't know me

as well as you think.
He said, *Hate to break it to ya, J,*

but I think I see
the you-est you.

BEING WITH COLIN FELT

like silence after sound—
the TV turned off

mid-commercial,
the headphone removed

post-run. It seemed
we transported

to some time and place
foreign to the clutter

of noise. Together
there was only us.

CAN YOUR GIRLFRIEND BE SOMEONE YOU'VE KNOWN A FEW DAYS

who lives on another continent?
he asked Becca one day, a sly smile
in my direction. I laughed.
He inched his rickety bar stool
toward mine. *But really,*
can I call you my girlfriend?

Labels leave a residue, I joked,
anthills blooming in my veins.

Only if you plan to peel them off—
otherwise, they're handy, Little J.
He made an example of himself,
a grab bag of name tags:

Colin, 18, straight Irish male,
employee of the Lemon,
boyfriend-hopeful of Little J.
He said, *Can't she, straight American*
backpacker, be girlfriend to me?

The stone pine above us poured shade
like lemonade from a pitcher.

One, I said, *Little J, Jenny, Jennifer,*
might be different people, if just slightly.

Two, there are as many ways of being American
as there are brands of peanut butter
on a supermarket shelf.

Three, am I a backpacker
when I'm not backpacking?

And four, I smiled,
I'm not straight.

He shook his head—*What? Wait—*
gave a big guffaw—*ha!*
then sloshed his beer
toward mine—*Okay, cheers,*
Little J, my great surprise,
to books n their covers n shite.

LATER, AT THE NEXT-DOOR DISCOTECA

having a nightcap with Becca, she leaned over the beat
and yelled, *So, you're bisexual?!*

Can't hear you! I gestured and kept dancing,
uninterested in explaining myself, unsure
if I was about to lose a friend.

She nicked her chin toward the door
and I followed to stand unsteady
on cobblestone in lamplight
and plumes of secondhand smoke,
where she asked again.

I gave my same refrain—*I hate labels,*
that one especially. The "sexual" in its name
kind of ensures I'm seen that way—really
I just think bodies are irrelevant shapes.

Jenny! She swatted my shoulder.
You could have told me. That's a big deal.

I stiffened—*Is it? Sorry I forgot*
to wear my billboard—but softened under
the boisterous arm she slung
like a warm shawl over my shoulders.

THE NEXT DAY

Colin covering a shift
for someone sick,
I found myself alone
in Villa Borghese.

Afternoon sun sliced
through leaves, piercing
the grass, darting across it
like centuries of footsteps.

Flowers strummed
their meandering pastels,
drummed bright bursts
of silence. All day
I eavesdropped,
my heart a fist unfurling.

I RECALLED IN CONTRAST

the crypt we saw,
the churches,
cathedrals.

I remembered very young,
my dad's words: *Travel is church.*
My mom's: *Just be good people.*

I thought of Colin crossing himself,
the curve of his fingers, the swish of his hand,
beautiful with what seemed

an innate gesture. *(Lapsed Catholic,*
he'd joked, *but don't tell me mam.)* I thought
of my freshman year of high school,

reborn (from a pretty secular Protestant)
in a Pentecostal church I attended
with a friend. I'd clapped

and danced and prayed in my skirts
for three incipient weeks filled
with the uninhibited adrenaline

of music, movement, touch—
emotional fuel so rare
it felt holy—naïve

to the tenets of the church,
until my parents attended with me once
and said, *Yeah . . . no.*

There in Rome, I looked
around me and thought—*this:*
the sound of a green leaf landing

on the steps where I sat, pink buds
peeking sleepily at sunlight
from a nearby bush. No dim

or dancing pews with manmade books
and human translation, but *this,*
the expanse of the wide world under the sun.

This, I thought, *is my religion.*

ON MY LAST DAY IN ROME

we started drinking at 9 a.m.
Colin kissed me as our glasses clinked

in a narrow, sunlit alley.
Teetering on the edge

of my wrought-iron chair,
I was anxious to breathe him in—

to get my fill before I'd have to say
goodbye. Sugary bubbles, sour juice—

the moments passed
bittersweet, one sip at a time.

THE COLOSSEUM A SPINDLE

we spooled again like thread,
Colin counted the eighty lower arches

in Irish because I loved the sounds,
and we stopped at every few Tuscan columns

to sew ourselves into it,
to kiss, to stand on solid earth

in each other's arms. We wove
through the Forum's scattered stones,

a flask passed between us, trying, I think,
to feel everything, but numb it, too—

the fact that we'd found each other
but wouldn't be together soon.

Cloud-gazing in Palatine grass,
we fell asleep, woke to meet Becca

for a movie, a boozy dinner,
a farewell night of dancing.

MY LAST NIGHT, A MEMORY

I don't prefer—left long unparsed
    and unsure—a fray, a fracture,

in the fairy tale. Stars slipped
    that night from our shadows

into the dank dungeon room, silky
    and salted with sweat, clumsy

with drink. I giggled at our
    bonking heads, our bumbling

bodies, and like a door from its frame
    swung away, thinking we'd call it

a day. *I think we've had too much*
    to drink, I said. Tugging me back,

he laughed—*Sorry, Little J*—
    the soft sound a down coat

on cold words—*you will finish*
    what you started. A doe

in headlights, I did, laughing back,
    my hewn heart stinging.

MORNING WHISPERED

through the barred basement window,
    limoncello lingering on its breath.

I stirred, peeled my cheek from his chest.
    An hour left. I waved away the night's

dull blade, the question mark it carved
    inside me, and we hampered the line

to board the bus, him hugging me tight.
    I wish we didn't have to say goodbye, he breathed,

his lips a little love-chapped on my cheek.
    My American Dream, my Little J, I promise

I'll see ya yet. Even as the bus pulled away,
    his blue eyes, round and wet, held mine.

I'll never see him again, I thought.
    I watched him shrink, my throat a knot,

his hand a frozen wave.

COLORADO

AUGUST 2007

INFINITE AS STARS

were cars on I-25, raised Dodge Rams
rushing by with balls hanging from their backs.
My eyes unaccustomed, strip malls,
chain stores, portion sizes galore-and-more—
I'd come home to my high school slice of America—

to the world of a much younger Jenny.
You still have a curfew, my mom had smirked,
Miss Jenny-Gone-Wild, Miss Where-in-the-World-
Is-My-Child. She and Dad kept tousling my hair,
tension melting into the air, just glad to have me back.

IT HAD BEEN YOUR STANDARD

Jenny-Rissa-Foley kind of night—
Chili's, a movie, Village Inn pie,
Rissa's fork zooming
toward my French Silk slice.

What do you think you'd do? she asked,
the night's movie—*Knocked Up*—
on our minds.

Are you kidding? Foley laughed.
Jenny wouldn't hurt a fly.

I don't know how
or why, but out of nowhere
my throat went dry, hand
full-clam, fork slipping.
I realized my period
hadn't come.

JENNY . . . ?

Jen . . . ?

IT'S GOING TO BE OKAY,

Riss said,
eyeing the pink-plus'd
pregnancy test, coaxing me
from the bathroom floor,
her hand on my back.
Mine was clutched, instinctive,
at my center. *You need a snack.*
I'm throwing noodles on the stove.

I'm not hungry, I groaned.

Flopped on my childhood bed,
I felt sharp against its softness, slunk
from its bowed mattress to the floor.

You can't think straight
with a screaming stomach, she said,
and I can hear yours from here.
Gentle, maternal Rissa,
the soon-to-be nurse.

You're not thinking straight
if you think I want to be thinking,
I said, my stomach scorched,
my heart same-same, like a pot
filled, forgotten.

THE BARE MIND

often offered by an aimless drive
was what I wanted. Rissa and I were silent
as the Colorado road rumbled beneath
my old red Wrangler, an Iron & Wine CD
spat out into its case. I didn't want anything
trying to make me feel.

The mountains' lasso looped me,
pulled strong from where they stood up ahead
in the highway's outstretched hand.
I let them bring me in easy, hoping,
I think, for their strength—their secret—
to weathering the elements
and still harboring such absolute peace.

My mind fogged into what felt
like kin to prayer—vague, wordless hope
directed at the hills.

Finally we crackled to a gravel stop
by the sign for Horsetooth Rock.
We're in flip-flops, Rissa reminded me,
one brow raised, but she followed
as I slipped from the car, my limbs limp
as waterlogged leaves, my heart a littered trail.

I'M PREGNANT

I told Colin, my cordless
phone trembling
and slick in my hand.

Little J, I loved you
before, I love you
now, and I'll love you
after, he said, barely

missing a beat, clipping
the shortest long-distance
moment stripped of sound.

Only *after* hadn't yet
occurred to me, half
a world away from *now.*

AFTER

is a loaded word.

It splits things—
as intangible as time,
as pulsing as a heart—

in two.

THERE ARE TRAGEDIES IN THE WORLD

and this isn't one of them
is something my dad lovingly
liked to say to help me
keep things in perspective—
a failing grade, a busted knee,
a fender bender, a fight.

I hoped he'd say it
when I shared the news
and wondered whether if he did,
I'd think he was right.

SEX

in our house
had been mostly
an unsaid word,

taboo and awkward
from our mouths—
alluring S,

forbidding X,
the E easy
to pay no mind—

small arms blooming
from a steady spine.

SO I'LL BE HONEST–

I'm not embarrassed.
I told my parents
over endless breadsticks

at Olive Garden
hoping to keep things smooth
as dipping sauce.

I'll be honest. It could
have gone better,
could have gone worse.

WHY DID YOU HAVE TO GO

and spread your legs? The phrase
made my hair raise, my skin crawl
with the shame it aims at women.

I tried not to blame my mom
for a knee-jerk reaction
or for the notions she may have grown up with,
presuming they'd be passed along.
But those words burned like summer sun
when you forget it isn't only there
to warm you.

I'm lucky. I laid out the bright side.
I finished high school. I'm not fifteen.

I don't remember which parent said
That's what you call luck?

I don't remember which parent said
You can still have the life you want.

WHAT LIFE

did I want?
It surprised me,

its being
a question.

MOTLEY

is what memory I have
    of the hidden days
that followed—

    sheet-dark, fear-slicked,
heavy with gloom—

    as I shut myself
alone in my room
    circling my decision.

MY BEDROOM WALLS

I remember, bright white
like stuck and shiftless clouds

    that seemed to hold vastness
    in them like a taunt—soft

and rough as rind on the pads
of my fingers as I felt

        for any makeshift moor
        to steady me, to quell

the coming waves, to lift me
from the dark and waiting deep.

ONWARD

my favorite teacher
used to say—

Mrs. M, Ceramic Arts,
12th grade—

when a vase broke,
when a bowl toppled

at the wheel.
Onward

toward everything
I'd always wanted.

ROY ORBISON SPILLED

through the speakers like soda
and I was twelve again, slurping sugar
through a straw, watching
my parents dance to "Pretty Woman"
in our Dallas driveway, the beat
bouncing from our truck.
But I couldn't stay there long—

the song ended and I was back,
near numb, sitting next to Rissa
in the car with Dad and Mom
on our way to the clinic. I envied

the window its clarity, watched
beyond it the vast prairie sink
and rise. I mouthed toward my stomach
a useless *I'm sorry.*

THE CLINIC ENTRANCE

was lined with protestors,
white signs homemade
with bloody red letters,
pictures of babies
unborn. It's too hard
to phrase that any other way.

It would be a lie to say
it was easy to walk by them,
their words like lead,
the truth I felt
in what they said.
But I felt my own truth,
too, one not negating
the other.

Inside I cradled
those truths in my arms,
neither simple, neither right,
but one feeling more
like it belonged.

THE SONG THAT PLAYED

from the ceiling speaker
like a cruel joke, I remember—
U2, "With or Without You."

My fingers dropped
the stiff strings of my paper robe.
The kind nurse—tall, thin red hair,

green eyes—I remember—
taking my hand in hers.
It was still there when I woke,

the yellow walls wobbling around me.
She squeezed my fingers, said, *It's so nice*
your parents are here with you.

I remember trying to smile.
They're so mad, my dry mouth croaked.
My face, I noticed, was soaked

with tears I hadn't known I'd cried.
But they're here, she whispered,
squeezing me again.

WHAT I DON'T REMEMBER

is the drive home, how
the Colorado sky must have shone
like it always did, majestic blues
so paint-perfect my chest
would bristle with their pigment,
blanched clouds billowing
like the caught breath blown
from awed mouths across millennia.

What I don't remember
is the red Colorado clay—ochre afterlife
of ancient volcanic rock simmering
in the sun's rays—or the rocks
jutting and jumping jagged from earth—
orange, crimson, copper, wine.

I don't remember if, on the after-
drive, I even opened my eyes,
or began to grow the grooved bark
of a bristlecone pine, creating of myself
a shelter wholly mine.

AFTER

I slept for days, Colin calling
at time-warped hours
to check in, one night
asking me over the beat
in the lobby bar
to marry him.

I pulled the covers
back over my head, said,
I don't think I heard you right.

Ya gobshite!—he yelled—
I gotta call you back, J—
some eejit just pants'd me.

When he called back
a full day later, he asked
again. *I don't think so,* I said,
managing a laugh. At him,
or me, or the sorry situation
I'm not sure. *Well shite,*

he said, *that's Irish luck,*
clicked off with a *kiss kiss,*
chin up.

I QUESTIONED MY IDEAS

about luck, grilled my friends
    for their thoughts on fate.
Had I left on that flight home…

    Had I kept my initial Athenian plans…
Had my last night with Colin
    gone some other way…

An exhausting, pointless
    game to play.
I didn't regret my decision

    but I walked stringless
through a maze of what-if's
    counting the overseen exits

that would have allowed me
    not to have had to make it.
And even more, I felt guilty

    for all this *I*—that *I, I, I,*
was here to feel
    and whoever'd been budding

inside me was not.

As though I have a right

to be so sad, so lost,

in the deepest dark,

so selfish

is what I thought.

MY HEART NO LONGER

a red carpet unrolling toward my dreams, the future was hard to see—and that it needed to be built by this broken me—staggering. Things that, days before, felt difficult seemed suddenly plain, smaller worries altogether gone—creek water leaked from my palm—like soon so much would be—skills, memories, someone's just-spoken words pending response. Everything blurred behind bonfire heat, my new strange past the cut wood's kiln. I couldn't seem to ban my gaze from the flames, even as I'd come to blinking, dizzied, razed. I printed, taped by my bed, pictures of the sculptures I'd seen with Becca, those fractured, enduring marble women.

I CAN'T DO IT

I said, meaning
continue being,
meaning

continue bearing
the pain. Breathless
as a boulder,

shivering
as Pikes Peak,
my body coiled,

wreathed,
weak, a fiddlehead
fern.

Mom unsmeared
tear-wet hair
from my swollen eyes.

You can, she said. *Know*
how I know? Because
you already are.

THAT SMALL PHRASE

became my go-to,
my get-me-through
one hard moment
to the next. A quick tilt

of the rearview mirror
to spot my strength—
I can, I'd tell myself;
I already am.

WHAT WAS THE COOLEST THING YOU SAW?

Foley asked, two milkshakes between us
in a booth at Village Inn
the day I'd planned to tell him—

but his words, each time I tried,
(Jenny wouldn't hurt a fly)
became a door I left unopened.

What was your favorite place?
I scanned my memories, a race
to locatc an answer. I tried

to describe some sights,
but no words felt right, language
and me like passing cars.

He eyed me, said, *You don't seem*
like the same person anymore.
I chugged, shrugged, my lips lifted

in a pseudo smile—a gesture
I shared with the girl who'd left
a few months before. So much,

invisibly, within me had changed—
things I couldn't name, couldn't
even grasp. It just seemed

some old version of me had taken
her last gasp. I decided then
I'd give her berth in a quiet, inner cove

as I packed, mapped, drove—
off to a new start.

NEW YORK CITY

SEPTEMBER 2007

RAIN WRUNG

steamy city streets clean, or as clean
as city streets could get, New York
in September a gush of hot breath
from what felt like the underworld—
appropriate, the whole place lit
and littered with myth.

My apartment was a glorified closet
in a tenement building, floors adorned
with a century of scuff marks, dented
and sloped where there'd always been a bed.
And that was it—a place to rest my head,
a dinky sink, a half fridge, a cupboard
for my things, and in the corner
a little ledge to call a bath. *Bigger than*
a backpack, I thought, *not half bad.*

It belonged to an old friend
of my dad's, who was living in Oaxaca
in a VW van. *I'll be back*
when I'm fluido en español, he'd said—
she can skip the dorms till then.

MY BRAIN A TRAIN

stuck on a broken track, classes I'd looked forward to
for years were a blur. Best were the lectures, bright halls
where I blended into the bodies around me, just another
face smiling politely. Worst—Freshman Writing,
a windowless room tucked within the Bobst Library stacks,
20 chairs lining a long rectangular table, the professor
a poet, earnest, asking us to search and bare our souls.

Nope.

COUNTRY MUSIC ON THE SUBWAY

is weird, but the twang of sad songs
comforted me where I went, and too,
the weight of the round earth chipped away
so we could slip through.

On rotation, Rascal Flatts voiced words
I wanted to make mine—"I'm Movin' On"—
Rodney Atkins ushered me—"If You're Going Through Hell"—
and Jo Dee Messina shaped my face brave to say
"Bring On the Rain."

Sometimes that's the kind of sad I needed,
the kind with a beat that could keep my feet
pointed toward sunrise, all the while
I could imagine it: riding off one day toward sunset,
darkness flasked at my hip.

GRIEF

your moon,
empty days ebb

and flow slow.
On Sundays I rode

to Rockaway Beach,
learned the way

the sand's bare ridges
bend. I rooted out

the sharp shells,
the empties, the small

inhabited surprises.
When I pick up this thought,

no one crawls from it.
This one is heavy,

a healing
stone to skip.

Nudged, this one
burrows.

SMALL WORLD–

the three girls from Greece lived down
my East Village street, one of them connected
to a girl, connected to a guy, who got
my ink blot of a resume in the right hands
at a top marketing firm. 18, unexperienced,
I could be their part-time copy girl, unpaid.
Of course! I cooed, proud to think myself
ahead of my own game. I hustled from work
to class and back, hair worn straight, smile
worn wide. I packed a lunch each morning,
blacked out with the girls most nights.

THIS IS THE BODY

I inhabit
but feel as though I float above,

I noticed if I mistakenly
slowed down.

It has two arms, two legs, a head
of tied-back hair.

I observed it taking tests,
filing papers, pouring coffee
as though I was in it,
as though it needed nothing
it didn't have.

I was in awe
of how simple it seemed,
how it put one foot
before the other.
How a song might lift
from its tongue as though invoked,
as though it could go on
without me.

CRAMMED LIKE FRUIT

in a glass of sangria, the girls and I woke
in a lazy-limbed pile of morning,
booze-breathed from a big night.

My sleep-thick eyes were still shut
when Sarah, the singer, who always
woke bright as a grapefruit bite, said,
Jenny, you have to see Colin again!
He says you're his soul mate!

Panic squeezed me quick, almost
to pulp, eager to gulp me down
its dry throat. I'd never mentioned
Colin to them. I shot up to find
his unanswered postcards
fanned out in Alli's hands.

He saved up for a ticket, she read;
he's asking when he can visit
and why you haven't been online.

Erica clawed a card away—*Wait,*
Colin who?! I swallowed silence
as she read, let her answer her own question.
A devoted European mystery man? Um,
call him and make a plan!

I coached myself—*Don't shut down, Jenny,*
they're friends.

All my life I'd been an open book
but lately I didn't know why.
I hadn't grown shy, just protective, selective
of what breath I turned to sound
knowing that, no matter, the earth
would spin around.

COULD I

relive our electric week that once lit me like a lamp?

explain our final night cold river held behind a dam?

form words to shape the child we made but didn't have?

I tried. They were patient. We cried.

AFTER THEY LEFT

I finally replied—
    Sorry, Colin, for the crickets.

~~How come~~   ~~I wish~~   ~~Why~~
    I guess

come anytime? I just can't
    make any promises

as to what we'll find.

IN TWO WEEKS, SURREAL

as a Dalí desert, a yellow cab door opened
    and Colin stood on my New York City street.

Traffic, sirens, voices faded, and I heard,
    staccato, my own heartbeat. I knew

right away what I'd thought all along—
    his untethered smile wouldn't be

enough to button up the emotional miles
    or the nine months passed

since Rome. The feeling wore me
    like bad perfume—that our story

was as shut as the locket he brought me,
    that he was a relic I was unready

to unearth from a past life.

TENDER

and awkward, we saw the city, most things
a first for us both. We paused before paintings

at MOMA; entered Victorian villas
at the Met; posed with Times Square's

naked cowboy, Colin's grin wide, giving
the guy a piggyback ride. (*Think that's*

the most skin I'll get all week? Colin asked,
nudging me, then capsized with laughter

when I answered, *Probably.*) Enraptured later
by a Broadway matinee, he replaced walking

with dancing for days. On our due date,
we skirted the silver hem of Lady Liberty's

long dress, a nearby bird's unsung song
the only sound. On Ellis Island, Colin found

and felt the letters of his last name
inscribed on a steel wall. And in Union Square—

That's the craic, mate, mind if I jam?!—
he played the upturned buckets with a band

I passed by every day, and I laughed,
    suddenly lit by him. He said, *I saw that*

in your eyes, can you give it another try?
    but it was gone again as he came close,

a ghost in the breath between us.

AFTER HE LEFT

I ditched school,
called in sick
all week.

I sat with myself
alone
becoming nothing

but listening.
That I had taken something
I couldn't return

was my own echo
I couldn't unhear.
The choice

felt no less heavy
for being one I'd make
again could I hit

rewind, could I hit
rewind, could I hit
rewind would I still

be me? Would I
want to?

BETTER MOMENTS,

fleeting, in green park grass,
sirens
for songs, sun

reaching toward me
like a good friend's arm—
I thanked

my smallness—
that saving grace—
my breath

inseparable
from every other
breath, person,

plant, stone—
thanked the atoms
in the air so old

that they recognized me
as theirs, that they
would have me.

I THANKED

the atoms, too,
that though I felt then

like a shell turned
to sand,

what I was faced
with building

was a life
of my choosing.

LET'S FIND YOU

a boo, Sarah said.
Move on to move on,

Riss nudged. I met up
here and there

with likely first-rate
girls and guys, but I

was unavailable
with baggage to spare,

my interest in love
buried somewhere.

I kept the talk small,
the touch light,

a dearth of self to share.

I STILL LOVED

and mourned
    the Colin and Me

we'd been before our last night
    in Rome. In spirals

I wondered
    if I'd misheard, misread,

misunderstood that night.
    ~~How come~~   ~~I wish~~   why

did he tug me back   laugh
    speak to me like that?

~~How come~~   ~~I wish~~   why
    did I roll with it   laugh back?

Because my body bloomed
    a bruised memory

of the last time a boy gripped my arm
    like that?

I wondered if I could feel it
    as playful, not a red flag

hoisted. But in my heart
    I knew the answer.

Call it weakness,
    call it strength,

that next day
    on the bus, I'd quietly

(so quietly even I
    didn't know

what I was hearing)
    raised my white flag—

it was over.

ABOVE THE WHOOSH

of a therapist's dusty fan, the din of traffic
outside her window, I raised my voice.

I'm trying to decide—practically yelling—
if I'm super zen or majorly depressed.
I swear she swallowed a small laugh
as she gestured *go on.*

Crossing my legs on the stiff edge
of her sage-green couch, I said
I don't think it matters much
what anyone does—in the grand scheme,
we're blips on the radar.

She weighed, nodded, waited, said,
That sounds like depression to me.

I'D THOUGHT NEW YORK WOULD BE

an escape, a metal ladder leading away
from my blazing brick self. But it didn't
feel like a calling—it felt more like stalling,
like there was something bigger somewhere

that might matter more to me, that might
make me feel more like I mattered. NYU's
freshman core covered the world's antiquities,
stale photos of vibrant things that in those

closed rooms seemed worlds removed.
They weren't. Work-wise (still unpaid)
I'd "risen," but I didn't care who bought
what, who spent where. That was my boss's

job, me trailing her everywhere, taking notes
learning the ropes. But I just. couldn't. care.
Campaigns for soap, a wanna-be Coke, savory
mints, framed art prints, red-bottomed shoes—

I had the blues.

UNSTEADINESS

my steadiness, in some ways

I strengthened, learning

my constellations,

guiding myself through.

I became okay with okay,

with meeting new days eye

to eye, each an almost-blind

date, unsure what I'd feel

or find. I think, like I've now seen

a dead plant do, some light,

some shade, some water,

some food, without really

realizing, I regrew.

THINGS FELT UNFINISHED

and I was afraid they always might
until I opened a package one night
sent from Rome. Weeks had passed

since we'd talked on the phone
(a month since he'd left on a plane
back to Rome) but here was an album

of photos and poems—*American Dreaming,*
he'd titled it, in careful cursive loops
on the cover. One hoop of its three-ring spine

held a gleaming silver fourth—a Claddagh ring—
two hands, heart, crown—and near it, a note:
To remember what we had and what we didn't,

what we have and what we don't. Cheers,
Little J, may your years be great. xx Colin

THE PHOTOS

were new to me—moments he'd caught
with a disposable camera I'd forgotten.

Us in the Lemon lobby, grins grand,
Peronis in hand, Becca's thin fingers
sprouting peace signs above our heads.
I smiled, thought, *We* were *dumb bunnies then.*

Us walking around and around
the fragmented Colosseum. *Lento,*
largo, we described its crumbling, liking
the feel of the words on our tongues.

Us sneaking potato pizza into the movies,
Colin's full mouth mumbling, *This is how*
an Irishman survives in Rome.

And the photo saved for last—me,
candid, a black bird rising from my palm,
my body a layer of illusion in Livia's
painted garden walls. I searched myself
for the memory, listened for Colin's
bright laugh bouncing behind the lens.
Silence stood firm. This scene belonged
to him. In a flash—quick, but enough—
I saw the girl as he did. Not knowing
I'd forgotten, I remembered her.

THE LIFE I WAS LIVING

was not for me. It was from a movie,
or something written I'd read and thought
I'd wanted. Maybe something an old me
could have loved.

Some trip to Europe, my parents had said
that day at Olive Garden. True.

Central Park unfolded before me like a map
and I made myself walk to a playground
to hear the high-pitched laughter I usually
worked hard to hide from. That day the sound
was stone, my heart a knife I whetted against it.

Soon came Whitman
in my own quiet voice—

> *Gently, but with undeniable will, divesting myself*
> *of the holds that would hold me.*

By noon, I can't explain it, I'd bought a ticket.

I OPENED MY EYES TO SUNRISE

and I was part of it, high above
the earth in this thing with wings,
as close to a bird as I'll ever be.

I pulled and opened from my bag
for probably the fourteenth time
a note my parents had sent me.
I could hear the Garcia melody
in my head as I read—"Built to Last,"
the lyrics in my dad's slanted all caps.

When Ireland burst from below
my skin brimmed, a body of water.
I felt a spirit, gentle against me,
where the air had felt like absence.
I focused on that as we surged ahead,
severed clouds reshaping.

IRELAND

JUNE 2008

FROM A BOUNDLESS BULL

to a caterpillar cocooned,
joy's full scope had found me most
in the quiet moments I dropped everything
and heard the earth—my throat
a pond whenever I listened,
a green frog catching in it.

So I would channel that, I'd decided.
Eavesdropper among the ages—
new role, new goal—archaeology
classes on the Cork coast teaching me
how to lift stories from soil
with the soprano scrape of a trowel.

Layer by layer, slow, the centuries
told their swallowed secrets, unburied
from deep beneath bright grass, to be
bathed and held to the light in the lab.

I wasn't searching for gold, or Troy,
or my child—just holding fragments
of the past in my hands—a bridge
to lives lived and forgotten over time,
lives much the same as,
and different from, mine.

COMING! I CALLED

to the soft knock at my door—
Tegan, my age, met

at orientation the day before.
Day one, here I go! xoxo

I signed my note to Mom and Dad,
then clicked dark my inbox, its

friendly chorus of questions.
(Riss: *Will you see Colin?*

Foley: *Why didn't you tell me?*
Becca: *When can I visit?!*

My boss: *Are you coming back?*
Erica: *Where else will you travel?*

Sarah: *Is this your new path?*
Allie: *Like . . . Indiana Jones?!*

I laughed. Truth was, I had no clue—
or should I say—I knew

that plans just then
didn't suit me,

that I was following with trusting feet
the unspooling thread

held by an inner Jenny.)
Flinging on my sweats,

hustling toward the door, I pulled
from my pocket a postcard from Dylan

received my last day in New York.
On it: Victor Hugo lines that flew

inside me, then left, on their wings
my suddenly loosening breath.

ONE SOFT MORNING

a sieve at work in my hands, soil fell away
from what I sought—shards of pottery
from passage tombs—Neolithic portals

to the dimension of the dead, inside of which
gifts were left. But my Claddagh ring kept
distracting me. I won't lie, daily

I thought of that child—a girl, I imagined—
and often of her would-have-been dad.
Only I felt no longer so leaden and sad,

but grateful for what they'd given me.
The thoughts were not concrete—more a presence,
a steady sense, gravity to tide—emerald surf

breaking on the beach.

THAT NIGHT

memories arranged themselves
like wildflowers in a vase, fresh-cut
and fringed, under my thatched roof.

A breath of wind through my small
square window, my Van Gogh calendar's
petal-thin pages whispered awake

and I realized the date—the anniversary
of the day that I met Colin, arriving
in Rome unknowing each moment

was a bulb planted in a garden.
The dark sky jeweled above me,
I walked to the village pub, closing soon.

Inside, familiar voices hummed bright
as noon, and I waved, nestling into my favorite nook,
the stone corner by the fire where I often

read a book. For a while I watched
the arc and ache of flames, how easy
they came together, pulled away,

and sipped memories sewn
from that Roman day,
dark and sweet as Guinness.

PRESENT DAY

HERE, HOME, I

keep the ocean close,
    let it grip me, shift me
through time and tense.

    In a breath, the present—
a wave's cold curl above me—
    becomes the past—the wet suit

shucked from my skin.
    Edging the shore at sunset,
I pocket small reminders.

    My favorite: a quarter-sized
scallop shell, dove gray—
    dappled as a memory.

ACKNOWLEDGMENTS

This story is fiction—no characters are portraits of real people, and Jenny is not me. But Jenny and I do share many experiences, including a life-changing backpacking trip through Europe. I want to thank the many people who took me in and cared for me in various ways as I trekked with abandon after college. Sabine Kern, Lorenz and Louisa Kern, and Alexander Kern—vielen Dank. I look back on Loch life with Lieb aplenty, and my Deutschlish got ein bissen Deutschier thanks to you. Sandra, Jesus, Patricia, and Veronica Triviño—muchas gracias. My memories of Palma de Majorca are full of warmth, light, and Calçotada. Remi Reverchon—merci beaucoup. Your apartment was small and my suitcase was not. You're a real lapis lazuli for letting me leave it there for "maybe a week?" aka three months. Thanks, also, for taking me to your favorite French restaurant—McDonald's. Quin "Frank Abooti" Abbot, thank you for galivanting across several borders with me—and I'm sorry (I'm sorry, okay?!) that I ate pizza with my hands in that nice restaurant. Chris "Books" Bloomfield, thank you for inviting me to sleep in the shelves, for your hospitality and life lessons, even if you scoff at a little *zig-a-zig-ahh.* Luca Tempfli and family—köszönöm. How generous to welcome me, a complete stranger, into your home—a generosity I always associate with beautiful Budapest, often conjured by a steaming cup of tea. To Petra Jakovac, Martina and Simon Gračnar, and the late Jozica and Vlado Jakovac—hvala. My time with you was a blessing. So grateful to have had that—to have canoed on the Kolpa, to have shared a beer at Pavel and Katarina's kitchen table, to have fallen off Jure's unicycle.

Demeter from Bulgaria, thank you for saying hello on that overnight ferry and being my Naples 'n' Pompeii travel pal. When I see a rat, I still think of yours requesting belly rubs. Yellow crew, thank you for the home away from home. C, thank you for the emerald surf. Shannon Smith and Vanessa Sawtell-Jones, thank you for scooping me up and along, and Shannon, for being my bridge to Boston.

Like Jenny, I witnessed a shipwreck from the cliffs of Oia, Santorini that proved fatal to a father and daughter. I hope their mirrored presence in *Calling Me Home* reads with my deeply intended respect to their lives and memories. I wish them and their family peace.

I've loved poetry since I was little, since discovering an old book by James Whitcomb Riley on my family's shelves and turning again and again to the music and warmth of his poem "A Scrawl." What I love most about poetry is that it can evoke feeling without having to tell a story, without needing to provide context, without requiring logical sense to be made, because feelings are often illogical, and because sense is sometimes beside the point. Speaking of the point, mine is: I'd never considered myself a storyteller—in fact, I often said I wasn't one. Now here I am having written this story, so grateful to the many people who helped bring it to life, and to you, dear reader, for sharing in it.

I began writing this story after having my kids, who—by the sheer fact of their existence—sparked a shift in the way I approached writing. In postpartum throes and joys, I paused a focus on singular poems, trying something new, wanting to know that during nap time I could sit down with a pen and pick up where I left off.

The manuscript wouldn't have come to life without Sara Freeman, author and writing coach extraordinaire, who is truly a coach in the deepest sense of the word—someone who sees your potential, highlights your strengths, empowers and guides with slightest hand. Sara, you are magic. I don't think there was a single time you told me what to do, yet I always hung up our calls with clarity and renewed enthusiasm. Plus, you didn't so much as snicker when I asked, "So . . . how do I *do plot*?" Truly, I still cannot get over my luck at connecting with you. Insert emoji praise hands here. Thank you also to writer and writing coach Gemma Leghorn, whose insightful reading, sensitivity, and gentle guidance was a boon, and to Megan Tripp, who stepped in at the eleventh hour to offer feedback at a key moment when I needed it.

Thank you to my agent, Allison Hellegers, who loved this book from the jump and worked patiently with me through rewrites. Thank you for finding *Calling Me Home* its home, and for your support each step of the way. To my original Holiday House editor, Della Farrell, I could not have imagined a safer haven for Jenny and her world. You saw this book the way I wanted it seen; your thoughtful insights and suggestions made all the difference. I am so grateful. To my inherited editor, Alexandra Aceves, you made catching this ball in the air look easy—and then you made it a better ball. What an unexpected gift. Of course, it takes a village—thank you to everyone at Holiday House who worked on this book, from proofreaders and copy editors to designers and production editors. Rebecca Godan, an especial emoji prayer hands for your many last-minute catches. Thank you, Dana Lédl, for the beautiful artwork.

Thank you to my fellow poets and writers, and to the many teachers and arts administrators who have supported and inspired my writing. My MFA cohort at UNH may find recognizable material in *Calling Me Home*. I'm grateful to them, and to the grad faculty at the time—David Rivard, Mekeel McBride, and the late and singular Charles Simic—for their feedback on countless poems that ultimately morphed into this book, and to poet Amanda Lou Doster for telling me to never apologize for writing 500 poems on the same subject. Thank you to poet Matthew Zapruder, whose lines Jenny ponders in the Greek Agora (years before they were actually published)—for words that have shaped who I am, and for a supremely kind response to the star-eyed fan mail I sent upon first reading them in 2010. Thank you to my Mass Poetry family, including poets January Gill O'Neil and Michael Ansara, inspirations who have spent tireless years supporting poets and broadening the audience for poetry.

Thank you to my soul friends: poet Hannah Larrabee, whose kinship, support, and enthusiasm don't waver even when I disappear into motherhood for entire seasons, and whose feedback on one or two of the earliest versions of *Calling Me Home* was incredibly helpful on the poem level. Thank you to Jane Hunt Tucker and Noah Tucker, whose friendship is my happy place. I could just curl up in it like a pup forever. Janie, I meet you each evening in my heart to paint our nails with a backdrop of bad TV. Cameron "Coomy La La" Mathews-with-one-T, Andy "A Rock" Rosenthal, Ryan "Rybot" Talbot, and Chris "Cookie" Marcheso, thank you for keeping me keeled with laughter while also grounding me in deep conversation and understanding, be it from marathon training trails, Disney World, classrooms full of burgeoning artists, or bus station bathroom stalls. I'm so grateful for you all. Thank you Roni "GF" Garr, the inspiration for Rissa. Patrick "Petri" Foley, cheers with a brimming pitcher complete with straw.

Thank you to Chris Macios for supporting and encouraging me in the creation of this book, the telling of this story, in so many ways. Thank you for the gift of immersive time on seasonal writing weekends, without which I can't imagine this book would exist. Thank you for much more, not the least of which is your help in creating and raising my two favorite people. Thank you for being a top-notch dad and co-parent. We are so lucky.

To Mom and Dad, Betty and Kevin Becker, thank you doesn't cut it, but those are the words I've got. Thank you for supporting me in life and art. Thank you for instilling in me a sense of adventure with a side of caution. Thank you for practicing what I imagine were deep Lamaze breaths over half the things I've called to report throughout my life. Thank you for raising me with the mottos Jenny's parents have borrowed from you. Thank you for your patience, grace, humor, hard work, and love. Thank you for encouraging me to live my life and write this book without fear or apology.

To associate producer Brendan Toller, I'm dumbstruck at my luck for having found you. Thank you for the art you grant the world, both that you create (everything from *Danny Says* to Dust Hat to that unreal spaghetti limon) and that you inspire and support in others. That I get to be one of those *others* I don't take for granted. Thank you for reading this manuscript, for making time and space for me to edit at your dining room table, for talking out the knots of final revisions. This book is better for your care, for your nuanced and honest insights, as is its author. Thank you for all ways, always.

To Theo and Robert, loves of my life, I am so lucky and endlessly proud to be your mom. You two are the music playing in the roller rink of my heart, the raspberry at the end of my cheek kisses, the honey pool alongside my quesadilla. Thank you for sharing your hearts with me. I love you bigger than the universe, forever times infinity.

To Noula—my firstborn, our sweet lady and rightful queen—thank you for being the potbellied pig I always wanted. It's an honor to be one of your belly rub dispensers.

And to you, dear reader, once more—for the gift of your time and energy, for sharing in this story—grazie mille, efcharistó, opa!